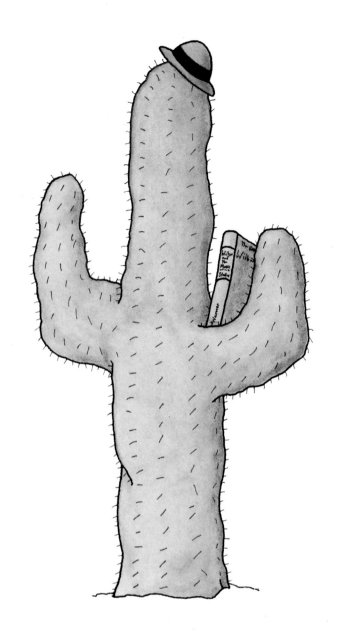

The Ballad of Wilbur and the Moose

By John Stadler

WARNER
JUVENILE
BOOKS

A Warner Communications Company
New York

Warner Juvenile Books Edition
Copyright © 1989 by John Stadler

Warner Books, Inc., 666 Fifth Avenue, New York, NY 10103

W A Warner Communications Company

Printed in Italy
First Warner Juvenile Books Printing: May 1989

10 9 8 7 6 5 4 3 2 1

Library of Congress Cataloging-in-Publication Data

Stadler, John.
    The ballad of Wilbur and the moose.

    Summary: A cowboy fond of lime juice and a big blue
moose work their way through a version of the Wild
West where rustlers steal pigs and the dealer in your
card game may be a crocodile.
    [1. West (U.S.) — Fiction. 2. Moose — Fiction.
3. Pigs — Fiction.   4. Stories in rhyme]   I. Title
PZ8.3.S7814Bal 1989   [E]   88-17349
ISBN 1-55782-047-3

To Norman and Simmy Klebanow

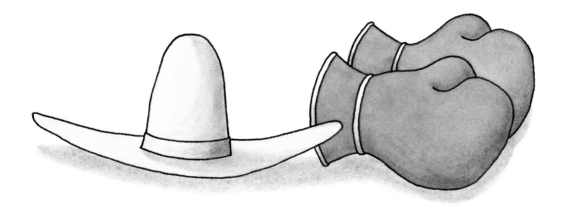

One night the cowboys were settling in around the campfire. "How about a song before we sleep, Whiskers?" someone asked.

The others agreed. So Whiskers pulled out his old banjo and sat back. He sang a song that went something like this:

Listen up, you cowpokes,
And I'll tell you all the tale
Of surely the weirdest cowboy
That ever hit the trail.

His name was Wilbur Little,
And he always drank lime juice.
He herded pigs for a living
And rode a big blue moose.

The moose, his name was Alvin,
A heavyweight boxer, they say,
Who knocked out everyone he fought,
And then called it a day.

Wilbur found him hitchhiking
And said, "Let's go out west.
I hear there's lots of pigs there,
And pig-herding's the best!"

They found a pig in Yuma
Above the desert sands,
Sitting on a cactus
With nine books in his hands.

He said, "I read all day long
Just in this position.
But if I sit here anymore
I'll need a good physician."

Wilbur said, "Come with us!
It's pigs that we adore."
The pig, he answered, "Certainly!
Besides, I'm getting sore."

There was a singing beauty
Who worked in a saloon.
She was a little piglet
Who couldn't carry a tune.

"Come with us," Wilbur said,
"And all that I request
Is that you do not sing again.
Then you can be our guest."

"I won't sing," the piglet said,
"And with you I do rejoice.
You see I really cannot stand
The sound of my own voice."

It was hanging day in Biddle's Creek
And the town was out in force
To see a pig get strung up
And let justice take its course.

"I'm innocent!" squealed the pig
As they lowered down the noose.
But suddenly from Nowheresville
Out ran a big blue moose.

He caught the pig upon his back
Just in the nick of time,
And welcomed him into their group
By offering him some lime.

They met a man in South Rock City,
A gambler by trade,
Who kept his own ten charming pigs
Locked up in a stockade.

He said to Wilbur, "Let's play cards,
And if I lose I'll pay,
With all ten pigs from the stockade
That you can take away."

"But if I win," the gambler sneered,
"I get your big blue moose!
And, in addition, I'll take control
Of all of your lime juice!"

Wilbur smiled and said, "Let's play,"
And sat down at the table.
The cards were dealt by a crocodile
Who used the name of Mabel.

The gambler leered and showed his cards:
Five aces and six twos!
But Wilbur smiled and said, "I have . . .
A big blue moose! You lose!"

They rode off quickly with the pigs
Won there in the bet.
But the gambler shouted from behind,
"You'll see, I'll get you yet!"

They found more pigs along their way
And offered each the job
Of walking 'round and oinking,
And eating like a slob.

So Wilbur started herding them
On a nifty piece of land
Between the brand-new railroad
And the mighty Rio Grande.

Now Wilbur loved his pigs a lot
And the pigs loved him right back.
So he and Alvin did all they could
To shield them from attack.

But the gambler found some pig-rustlers,
Who wanted hogs to steal.
He said, "Let's take ol' Wilbur's pigs.
They'll make a tasty meal!"

So they rode that night at a real fast clip
Out to Wilbur's place.
They rounded up them piggies
And left without a trace.

Daybreak came and Wilbur saw
That all the pigs were gone.
So he jumped on top of Alvin's back,
And cried out, "Moose! Ride on!"

Mines   - 1 mile
Rustlers - 1 mile
Pigs   - 1 mile
1 mile   - 1 mile

Alvin raced on out top-speed,
Following the signs
That led them to the rustlers
Held up in the mines.

The rustlers laughed right out loud
And said, "*This* will be fun!
One's a moose and one is weird
And doesn't carry a gun."

But Wilbur took his lime juice out
As he crept up sneakily
And poured the drink down on their heads
'Til they could hardly see.

Then the moose ran up and knocked them out
Before they could react,
And rescued all the piggies.
And that's, my friend, a fact.

So if you're out there on the trail,
And come across this sight:
A cowboy, moose and piggies
Riding through the night,

Don't laugh out loud or point, my friend,
Just move on slow down south,
Or you'll find you're full of lime juice
With a moose punch in your mouth!

Whiskers put down his banjo and looked around.

"How'd you like it, boys?" he asked.